IN THE DARK ROOM

Explicit & Forbidden Erotic Hot Sexy Stories for Naughty Adult Box Set Collection

Natalia Lars

This is a work of fiction. Names, character, places and incidents are either the product of the author's imagination or are used fictitiously, and any resemblance to actual persons, living or dead, business establishments, events or locales is entirely coincidental.

FIRST EDITION 2021

STORY 5

He had written her a letter and she knew how reluctant he was to do it. It wasn't much that was written on the cream-colored paper there: "I want to surprise you my beautiful one! Dress up and wait for me in front of the door at 8:00 p.m. "Her heart was pounding on her neck and she didn't know what to do. Her joy was all over her body, but at the same time she felt sick and felt terrible tingling in the stomach.

Terribly exciting and at the same time terribly beautiful. He wanted to surprise her, that is, she would see him and that, even though she was so far away from him. He would drive the 300 km for her. Her temperature became hot and cold at the same time .

After not seeing each other for four weeks, she would be able to look into his deep brown eyes again, stroke his chin, kiss the beautiful lips. She often imagined seeing him again when they couldn't see each other for several weeks because he was working and her studies kept her 600km away from him. Her internship at least shortened this distance a little. When she called him on the phone, she often closed her eyes, so he was even closer to her. She had often fallen asleep with the cell phone in her hand, which then stood for him.

Although he often said that he loved her more or thought more of her and missed her more than she missed him, she honestly doubted it a little. She loved him very much, right down to a silent "I love you!" Which she did not dare to say, because she feared he would not feel that way and narrowed down. Her acquaintance had not yet become so firm and grown she had shed a few tears because of him, but her personality also contributed to it.

She was afraid of losing him, something like that had never happened to her before. She enjoyed being in love, even if he sometimes did not know what he wanted But she believed in herself. She believed in: "You, me and we two!" and wanted to enjoy the time they had together.

So tonight he wanted to surprise her. Her grin would have run around her head once had it not been for the ears that naturally limited it.

This made working with the children even easier. It was fascinating what these little beings already had in terms of knowledge and skills. It was just as terrifying how this could be disturbed. The working environment was very pleasant, she was received very well there and she liked it very much.

All day long she had been pondering what she would wear for him that evening. She wanted to surprise him, she knew that.

After finishing work and bringing the last child to his parents, she went to her room. The treatment center had been kind enough to give her a room for the time she would spend her internship there.

She picked up the letter again, read it once, twice, and could not believe it. And then fear came. That unfounded fear that kept pounding her. She was looking forward to seeing him again, so much more with his announced surprise, but what if he canceled at short notice if he didn't want to see her. She didn't like it when fear came, when she became helpless. She didn't want it and yet the fear resonated a little. She tried to ignore it. If he treated her so badly, it wouldn't have been worth it. At the same time, however, she knew that there was no reason for it. Why should he have treated her badly when he kept telling her how much he loved her on the phone or telling her that he missed her.

Get rid of your thoughts, she said to herself!

She would have another three and a half hours before he would stand in front of the center and wait for her.

Your joyful expectation increased with the passage of time.

She went to take a shower! The warm water tingled on her skin. She soaped herself, stroked her body, massaged the shampoo into her hair and lost herself in the relaxation. Unfortunately, she didn't have a bathtub, but it was okay.
The razor ran over her armpits, stroking them more than letting them feel the blades. She watched him carefully between her thighs. She really liked it when her pubic was bare, smooth and velvety to the touch. Finally, the legs that she later wanted to dress in skin-colored stockings. She was just washing the conditioner out of her hair, "mh, how good it smelled."

A towel was wrapped around her head and she dropped onto the bed, too. Drying a little and relaxing.

When she thought of him, she grinned. The tingling sensation went through her whole body again.

She fell asleep with a smile. The vibrating of an SMS had woken her up. He had sent her one of his typical messages "rabbit" no more. But he wasn't there yet. She had slept for about an hour and now had some time, to be exact, two hours. Her hair wasn't quite dry yet, but it was There was still time, she washed it a little dry and then combed it.

The cream with olive extract caressed her skin, she enjoyed the tender, soft feeling. She did something good for her body and hoped that she would like it afterwards.

After touching every inch of her body and growing her excitement just by doing so, she brushed her teeth. Quite unotic, but necessary. She loved fresh breath and when she could run her tongue over her smooth teeth. She already felt fantastic when she looked at herself in the mirror. Now a little makeup.

She powdered her face a little, not much, just a little. Then she carefully framed her brown eyes with black eye pencil. Magic big shining eyes, they were big anyway, but so they came into their own even better. In addition, the eyelashes were washed deep black. She thought smoothly of falling in love with herself. The icing on the cake was the colorless lip gloss she loved so much. He made her lips shine so beautifully moist. Made the subtle makeup perfect.

Now she could also look after her hair. She leaned forward, brushed her hair out, and sprayed a little hairspray into it to give them a little momentum and volume, not too much. It should still be natural and should not be concreted. If he ran her hair through it should feel soft, they should be supple.

What can be described here so briefly and simply did take some time. The eyeshadow could drive you crazy. In the end, however, she was satisfied with her result.

She also knew exactly what she wanted to wear. She smoothly pulled a black thong over her hips, which was only available on special occasions, and this was a special occasion. For this she put on the black strap corsage, whichwas padded on the straps and the breasts with a little pink fabric, plus a small lacing in front of the belly. She loved corsets of all kinds. She liked that feeling, the severity and a little bit the tightness. When she wore it she walked upright. Now it was the turn of one of the sanctuaries. The skin- colored shiny nylons. She knew he loved her and that was the only reason why she had bought her. Slowly and gracefully, she pulled the fine stocking over her left foot first, then up over her calf, all the way up to her thigh, where she fastened it with the suspenders. Her right leg also enveloped her in this seduction.

Before she pulled the black dress with the colorful flowers printed on it over her shirt, she put on a little deodorant. The dress reached to just above her knees on one side and was cut a little longer on the other side. If she would get into the car afterwards, she would have to be careful not to let the dress slide too high. Or maybe that was exactly what was wanted.

Now it was almost perfect. She had often imagined dressing up for him. To make him happy, to surprise him.

A little more perfume. Armani Code was a heavy fragrance, but it suited her! He lay down on her hair, her neck, her arms. She loved him. Draw the lip gloss again a bit, done. In a small pocket she put her ID, a little money, two handkerchiefs, the lip gloss, a small metal tin with condoms, and her cell phone. The room key would be added later.
She was nervous, terribly nervous. She still had a quarter of an hour. Now perfection should be

achieved. She knew how much he loved skin-colored stockings. But he loved high heels at least as much. Preferably made of black leather. But why exactly made of black leather!? Maybe you can think of an explanation.

They were high heels with a heel of fifteen centimeters. She found a lot, a lot for a woman of her size. So she could easily look him in the eye. With these shoes she was about 1.95 m tall. The leather closed around her feet. She closed the strappy, carefully, full of expectation. Up until now she had only carried them around the room and was wearing them for running in. She walked back and forth through the small room and the clicking of these shoes was surely heard across the hall.

So she was standing in the middle of her room, at a dizzy height, with her head raised and an insane stance.

She opened the door, stepped out, and locked it behind her.

It was a little uncomfortable for her to walk through the clinic, after all, there were people who were barely able to walk, old and sick, people in need of care. The more she hurried on her way.

Outside she received the warm evening air of an early September evening. It would probably be cool later, but she didn't think about it.

As the letter had commanded her, she stood at the door. She stood in front of the treatment center in her black shoes and dress, looking out. Look for him or his car. But nobody was to be seen yet.

At some point she looked at the watch impatiently. It was often impatience that grabbed her when she longed for his attention or wanted to see him, but waited in vain for a message from him. Her cell phone indicated that it was five minutes past 8 p.m. Where was he Should her fear have been justified? The glow faded a little from her eyes as time progressed. But she didn't force herself to call him to patiently endure whatever came.

She sat on a bench. Don't try to cry, don't be too disappointed. But that was difficult. So hard.

When she was looking at her cell phone again, he came around the corner. The glow and excitement returned to her body. She put the phone away and got up, straightened her dress and took a few steps towards him.

He stopped and just looked at her. The wind carried some of his perfume over. He had put it on for her because he knew how fond she was of that smell. Simple and classic only Mexx. All that was needed to make her happy.

It was a dream as it stood there in front of him. Her bright eyes, the gentle smile that even showed her teeth. So real, so lovely, so exciting. And what she was wearing. The hammer. These shoes! He had no idea that she called such a couple her own. He loved her. Only he had never told her quite consciously.

She walked towards him in these high shoes. No insecurity, no hesitation, insanity. Her arms wrapped around his neck and he grabbed her around the waist. He couldn't greet her with more than one deep throaty "baby". She sighed in his ear, pressed tightly against him and he took in her warmth, her smell. This heavy sensuality.

She secretly wiped a tear from her eye. She was relieved that he had still come. She was happy to see him again. She felt her heart beat as if it wanted to jump out of her full chest.

He kissed her gently on the cheek. "Come on my darling!" He said and took her hand. They went to his car and he even opened the door for her. She beamed at him. If stars were already visible at that time, they would have sparkled with her can.

She had so much to say and at the same time again nothing. She wanted to be. just enjoy his presence only with him, feel his warmth. hold his hand.

Before he got in the car, she had time to straighten her dress so that he didn't see that she was wearing suspenders..He should only find out later.

He looked so damn good in his black shirt and dark trousers and shoes. She had never seen him like this before. Otherwise he wore polo shirts and jeans or normal pants. But tonight seemed really special.

She stroked his smooth-shaven chin, turned his face to hers and gave him a careful, short kiss on the lips. After such a long time, she needed a little bit more before she could give herself completely to him, before she could stroke his neck, when the tongues played with each other and the lips pressed together.

She would also have liked to feel his beard. She didn't care if he was smooth and tender like a baby's bottom or if he had a beard that scratched her a little while kissing, but it didn't make the whole thing less attractive.

He was he and that was a good thing. His corners and edges, his peculiarities and quirks made him what he was and exactly this mixture fascinated her so much, even though they hadn't known each other for half a year.

In this area, he should have known less than she did, and yet he purposefully drove his way, while his right hand kept finding the way to her left thigh.

He drove to the pampas with her. Okay, that was not difficult. She was actually there already, but he kidnapped her to an even more remote corner of the country. The view of the Alps was breathtaking. He stopped the car in a remote parking lot.

He grabbed her, hugged her and kissed her. Without contradiction. You surely know this quiet groan of surprise and pleasure. Exactly that moan slipped from her throat as he held her and kissed passionately. She pressed against him and her hand curled the back of his neck.

First of all, she had weak knees when someone kissed her. That was with him after they hadn't seen each other for almost eight weeks and were really kissing for the first time. It was worse this time. Her knees got really soft, she staggered a bit backwards and stopped at the car. He released the kiss, but continued to stand very close to her, looking into her eyes, stroking her cheek and noticing her violent breath. He was just breathless and happy.

She knew it had excited him. She herself was very excited about this kissing. Only the excitement was not to be seen. With him she pressed against her pants. It promised to be a very pleasant evening.

He blindfolded her, then got something out of the trunk and took her by the hand. Walking through nature in these shoes was not that easy, but he held them. Hold her hand and lead it!

"Wait a moment!" He said, leaving her standing there in the darkness. She heard it crackling and rustling, then he took off her blindfold. On the floor there was a blanket and a few pillows, next to it was the basket in which he was everything had carried here. He sat down and laughed. She sat down and just enjoyed his proximity.

The dress slipped a little and released her leg a bit. His eyes fixed on herand then he pulled her close , kissed her and kissed her on the floor.

It was good.

She turned him on, was beautiful and sexy at the

same time. He had seen that she was wearing the stockings he liked, but the shoes were awesome. All the while, his excitement was pressed firmly against the fabric of his pants.

He wanted her, he wanted her, had missed her all weeks! He just hugged her in his arms, she was sitting in front of him and leaning against him.

"I love you so much!" She whispered out into the evening and his lips approached her right ear as he whispered: "I love you more!"

They sat silent for a while, enjoying the peace and quiet and the closeness of the other. It could have stayed that way for her. She didn't want to let him go. And he didn't leave her alone either.

They both snuggled up on the blanket, it was in his arms, looked at him, only briefly, because then they kissed again and he pulled her tightly to himself.

She put her left leg behind his body to get even closer to him. She liked what she did and what he saw, the stockings held up by the suspenders. And he liked what he felt, a bare bottom, soft, velvety buttocks that seduced him to touch her with a light blow.

When she put her hand over his pants, he stopped

her. "Not yet! We have time! Come on! "And he pulled her up to him. What else was he going to do with her? She helped him clear the pillows and the blanket and he took her hand again as they went back to the car.

Her goal was unknown, but it didn't matter. He had kidnapped her, he was allowed to do that today, she trusted him deeply.

He was so cute, so beautiful, so sexy and at the same time a man through and through. He gave her security.

They stopped in a city in a parking lot and he led them through small streets. The fact that his hand made an excursion to her rear again and again did not bother her a bit. She enjoyed the tenderness as much as when he kissed the back of her hand.

He should have done anything with her.

The people on the street watched them go. Was it that unusual? But she just smiled and he was glad that she was there.
The click of her shoes gave him goose bumps, it was a dream.

He had chosen an Italian. Small and cozy! The white wine made her cheeks rosy and you could see how she enjoyed the food. How her full lips wrapped around the noodles and she slowly sucked them into her mouth. How her tongue licked the rest of the sauce out of the corner of her mouth, just how she was sitting there, that made him insane. Not to mention the foot that slid up his trouser leg under the table. Can you imagine what that triggered in him !?

He wanted to take her. Swept the candles and plates from the table, placed them on the table, pushed her dress up and sunk his excitement past her thong in her hot, wet paradise. Unfortunately, this was not possible. Respectively, he did not want to get excited by public annoyance.

He paid and they stepped out into the cool dark night. They laughed and strolled through the city together! Then kissed each other, gasping for air. It was a nice tingling, an electrifying, intoxicating feeling. Again his hand found the way under her dress, between her thighs to her moisture. She moaned softly in his ear and pressed her pelvis against his finger.

She felt the freshness as he wriggled his finger out of her and shivered. Before returning to the car, she savored her pleasure with pleasure. You drove him crazy!

He had a sweater for her in the car, and she accepted it with thanks. She liked to carry his things. They were so familiar, smelled so good, and warmed twice as well. He looked at her questioningly: "Are you sleeping with me in the hotel?" A smile settled on her lips before she leaned over to him, took his face and kissed him passionately. "Then let's go!" and so they flew through the silent night.

She didn't know he was on vacation, but it had to be that way, otherwise he couldn't have stayed. It didn't really matter, the main thing was that he was there. He let her climb the stairs to the room first, so he could look at her bottom, her legs, her hip swing. When he grabbed her from behind, she had to laugh and he covered her mouth. After all, other guests were also present.

The hotel was very nicely decorated. A large firm bed, a private bathroom with bath, shower and sink, very elegant and well-kept, even a small kitchenette was to be found. But none of this really matters.

No sooner was the door closed than she leaned against it and pulled him close and kissed him like there was no tomorrow. He kissed her back, kissed her neck, to her ear, and back again. That drove her crazy, it excited her, made her moan softly and lustfully. His lust pressed against her pelvis, pressed cheekily and shamelessly against her. "I want you!" She said to him, without frills, without flowers, just "I want you!"

He didn't hesitate for a second, locked the door and dragged her onto the bed with him. He was kneeling over her, afraid to hurt her. In doing so, she assured him that she would enjoy it when he was lying on top of her and that she could feel his weight. He complied with her request, but then slowly kissed deeper, stroking his big, beautiful, strong hands over her breasts, over her belly, down to the thighs. She had bent her legs.

To take off her panties he would have had to undo the suspenders. So he pulled her back on her feet and removed her dress and took the shirt with her. So his dream woman stood there in front of him, the heels on the feet, the legs in the sexy stockings, held by the suspenders of the corset.

He took a few steps back to look at her and she started to pose. Laughing, he turned in a circle, looked at him boldly, stuck his buttocks out or crouched lasciviously with his legs spread wide so that he could see where the string had gotten a damp stain.

She stretched herself up to then walk up to him, turn him around and push him onto the bed. She knelt over him. A picture for the gods and his excitement finally wanted to see it live. She kissed him, coaxing a comforting groan as she sucked on his earlobe and ran his left hand into his lap, over his hard pleasure.

Now she opened the shirt button by button, slowly, very slowly and kissed the piece of skin every time, which was more apparent. The pants followed the shirt. He felt miserably slow, but at the same time so indescribable.

At last she had taken it off completely and was able to look at him as God had created it, strong and well built with the thighs of an athlete, which fascinated her again and again. He groaned for the first time as she put her lips around his swollen glans. With relish, she began to suck his cock deeper, to suck on it, as she did with the soft ice cream. She licked and smacked and sucked and sighed as much as she could while her wet lust kept sliding over his knee.

He wanted her!

"I want to lick you!" He interrupted her pleasure and she got up. Positioned herself in front of the bed and started to loosen the suspenders. He should see everything exactly. She took a lot of time as she slipped the string over her buttocks, stretched out to him and spread his legs a little more to let him see her wet glitter, and after she had put the suspenders back on, she went back and forth a few more times for him, presented herself, then stood around to look around kneeling over him.

He pulled her pelvis onto his face, his tongue searched for the sweet pearl and started to play with it while she moaned lustily in his lap. She hadn't been allowed to enjoy such touches for a long time. In order not to fixate on her orgasm, she started to massage his lust with her tongue and used her hands to pay a visit to the two friends while she sucked and massaged, he licked wonderfully. He made her go up the steps of excitement.

Just a moment and then she had reached the cliff and crossed it. Everything in her head was turned off and only the moaning stopped. Her body twitched, went through a thousand small electric shocks, and he licked her juice.

Licked through her column and made her wince again, again and again.

Sex was not only fun, it was also exhausting. She was panting and sweating and yet was in another world, lifted off for the moment.

He pushed her aside, stroked her hair and pulled her towards him. Pulled her on her shaky legs and undid the suspenders and then he opened the corset one by one until she was standing in front of him in stockings and shoes. He stroked her back and leaned forward so that she could support herself in the kitchen alcove. A wonderful sight, the bottom stretched out, the shame, bare and unrestrainedly moist, inviting, very inviting.

So he directed his manpower between her thighs and was greeted by a pleasant heat. It was tight and with every thrust with which he pushed forward she tightened around him in the aftermath of her orgasm. A feast. Slowly he began to push her, calmly leisurely and each push made her shake and groan. He stroked her back up to the back of her neck, grabbed her by the neck and slowly directed her upper body towards him. Her breasts swung in time with his thrusts and her nipples became rock hard as he ran his thumb over them.

The last time, and at the same time the first time, she had wished that he should take her until he came. This wish should be fulfilled today. He was more excited than he had been in a long time. His bow went in and out, was about to burst. His pace was murderous and the tones of bare skin on bare skin mixed with the hoarse groan. When she leaned forward a little and then sucked on his fingers, it was all about him. His neurons fired uncontrollably, made him intoxicated when it came to him, that he gave everything he had to her. And she took in his twitch with delight, pressed himself a little bit towards him and enjoyed his quick hot breath that brushed the back of her neck.

She let him slide out of her, turned to him and kissed him passionately again. "Come on, we have to sleep, the night is going to be short!" And so she pulled him to the bed. He knelt like a prince before her and undid the straps of her shoes, took them off her feet and took off her stockings from her legs.

A kiss here and a kiss there, the fire was far from extinguished, and together they crawled under the covers, snuggled together a little, his hand caressed her side, her breasts, her belly, and his mouth kissed her neck press hard against him last time, feel his closeness and then she fell asleep, and he was also kidnapped a short time later in Morpheus' realm.

In his sleep, he mumbled something as he held her hand firmly, which sounded like an "I love you!" And she murmured softly and drowsily back, "I love you too!"

The End.

STORY 6

I woke up because the Ibiza sun burned on my backside. I was alone on the beach. On my first day of vacation. Richard, my partner - or rather my ex-stage partner - should have been lying next to me, but we had split up just two days before the vacation.

"Cara," he had said straightforwardly. "I noticed that I am bisexual." "What?" He shrugged. "I fell in love with a man."

"WHAT!?!"

"That doesn't change our relationship. I even think it can enrich them. There could be three of us ..."

When Richard started to argue, it was all too late. "OUT!" I roared. "Get out of my apartment. I do not want to see you. Never again! You - you tune! "

Five minutes later, I was crying on the sofa with a large sundae. A sleepless night later, I decided not to let my planned vacation spoil me. I was thirty, kept fit, and looked good. I would quickly find another guy. One who didn't sleep with other men.

When I got here on the beach, a large palm tree had

given shade at the edge. But now the sun had moved on, and I either had to find another place - which was no longer so easy - or I first went into the water.

On the way there I let my eyes - camouflaged by big sunglasses - roam the small groups.

Hmmm. Families with children, individual "gentlemen", groups of young people, two - My step stalled. Two guys my age. Well-toned bodies, short but not too short hair, friendly faces. Very appetizing tight and well-filled swimming trunks. One with very fair skin and reddish hair, the other either very tanned or naturally dark.

I continued walking towards the water and kept an eye on them from the corner of my eye. They talked to each other, the dark man took a bottle of sun milk out of his pocket and began to smear the light man's back. Good friends.

But then I almost tripped over a grain of sand. Crap! Tunten again.The Dark had bent down to first kissed the neck of the light, but then the head had turned, and now making out the two together. I could only shake my head.
Already lost two tails for the women's world.

My feet got wet, so I must have reached the waterline. The beach ran very flat into the sea here, so I could keep walking straight for a while. In the distance a large cruise ship ran parallel to the shore ... maybe I should have gone on vacation with something like that.

I continued my path thoughtfully. Sure, a beautiful male body was probably not just an appetizing sight for a woman. Just like I also appreciated an appetizing female body. But you didn't have to jump into the box with someone just because they looked good.

I was up to my thighs in the water when a movement startled me. Oh shit! The steamer pulled a bow wave behind it that was not from bad parents. She approached me almost head high. I took a step back, another, stumbled, rowed with my arms, and the water was already there.

A blow, as if a car had hit me, pulled me off my feet. Suddenly I no longer knew where was up and down

, I held my breath with all my might and tried to find a hold ... Strong arms grabbed me and lifted me until my head came out of the water and I could gasp for air.

"Are you okay?" Asked a worried male voice with a very erotic timbre. "Y-yes," I coughed. "Thank you, ...?"
"Daniel," he said.

I looked at him. It was the dark one. Damn it! "Thank you, Daniel." He slowly put me on my feet, but kept his hands under my arms.
"If that makes you uncomfortable, you can let go of me," I blurted out.

He frowned. "Why? Why shouldn't I want to hold on to such a handsome woman?" He looked around briefly. "Or do you have your husband with you?"

"I thought ... Sorry."

He had seen my sideways glance towards his place and grinned. "You saw Tom and I kissing?"

"Uh ... yes."

"We are not gay." "Oh!"
That should have been clear to me by now. His hands were still holding me still, but his eyes flickered to my breasts, which were only partially covered by my bikini top after the water hammer.

And did something stir in his pants? Well ... "Thank you Daniel for saving my life." I stretched up to his feet and kissed him on the mouth. With closed lips ... for now. Hmmm, coconut flavor.

He didn't back away. The pressure of his hands tightened and he pulled my body against his.

"Can I," I murmured, "prove my gratitude in any other way?"

He looked at me and a smile stole into the corner of his mouth. "I already knew something there."

"Are we thinking of the same thing?" I furtively moved my lower body, felt something hard in his swimming trunks. "Doesn't ... uh ... Tom mind?"

"Not if he can participate," came a slightly higher voice from behind me. "But maybe we should go behind the ledge."

My God! I never dreamed of that. "Yes" was all I could croak out.

Daniel reached under my knees and lifted me up. I could just hold on to his muscular neck and we were already moving.

His mouth found mine again, and this time I opened up to him. It tasted of salt water and man. Fantastic.

Hands lay on my buttocks. Vigorous hands that started massaging me. Fingers slowly working their way forward, pushing my lower part to the side and reaching my labia.

I sighed. Daniel turned me off. My hands were finally free, I pulled off his swimming trunks and a handsome tail jumped towards me. "Oh," I said. "Appetizing." Then I held on to his bum, I leaned forward, opened my lips and took his crown into my mouth.

I had never had a cock in my mouth that tasted of the sea. The taste surprised me, but not negatively. "Hmmm," I said, and the tail bounced.

"Oh god," Daniel groaned. His hands lay on my shoulders.

Tom's hands left my butt - judging by the rustle, he put on a condom. It only took seconds, then his hands were back, pulling down my bikini bottoms. I spread my feet further apart and felt my labia open. My pussy was ready as I was. I released Daniel's cock for a moment. "Take me, Tom." And then back again. At the same moment, Tom pushed from behind, and Daniel's cock slid deeper into my throat than I had ever dared.

Oh my god, what a feeling of being filled from

above and below. I wanted to take a breath, realized that it was not going to work, but both of them retired.

"Ahhh!" I groaned as soon as I could breathe. "Go on, hard—" But that was it. In - out - air - "Ahhh"

"You should be a little quieter," Daniel murmured tightly . "There are people just around the corner."

But I didn't care. The next time I pulled out, I let my teeth slide over the tail, and Daniel acknowledged that with a "shit" that was definitely louder than my moans.

In - out - air - "Ahhh" I don't remember how many times we repeated this, but I felt that the tail in my mouth started to boil. Soon he would ... And already he felt poured into my mouth indefinitely; Tom hit him hard again, and then he and I came too.

*

It was early evening before I was back in my hotel room and able to make calls.

"Richard," I said, "can you forgive me? I ... I want to meet your friend." He took a breath, hesitated. "And," I continued. "You will get what you always wanted from me. Or you two together."

The End.

STORY 7

It was another hard day. I had meetings all day at my company's headquarters. Sometimes these regular business trips to Kiel got on my mind. I always lived first class, but it was no comparison to living at home.

For my free time in the evening, I had discovered a small bay here in which hardly anyone was staying. Here I could sit on a bench and comfortably process my mail on a table. So I switched on my notebook and delved into my electronic mail. No human soul was here, and although the bay was only ten minutes from the hotel, the calm was only disturbed by the sound of the sea. During a break I closed my eyes and let the sun shine on my face.

Then I heard a slight sob diagonally behind me. 'I'm here alone today,' I thought, looking around. At the end of the path on the last step sat a little bundle of misery. It had its head on its arms and was crying. I took a closer look at them. On her back she had a backpack that looked bigger than the wearer. Her head was covered with a baseball cap, out of which black streaked hair looked out. Her sweaty t-shirt ended just above her shorts. The first tears dripped onto her dusty legs, leaving dark streaks until they were picked up by her small, dirty sneakers. I estimated it to be about twenty years

old.

I went to her, bent down to her and asked, "Can I help you?" She looked up at me. I looked into a dirty and tear-stained face, but it still looked very cute.
Her brown eyes looked at me, eyed me briefly and shouted: "Are you such a married pervert trying to rape little girls!" Desperate anger was in her eyes now.

"Excuse me, I didn't want to get too close to you," I replied startledly. Without further words I went back to my table and continued to process my emails.

Half an hour later she was sitting across from me on the bench, looking at my bottle of cola and the biscuits that were on the table. I ignored her at first and then said without looking at her: "You can get hold of it if you want, only I have no glass and have already drunk from the bottle." I had hardly said it when she drank from the bottle and the biscuits disappeared one after the other, leaving a sip of Coke and that from a large bottle, and as greedy as she had been drinking, she had almost died of thirst and had been without food for a long time.

"Thank you," she said. But she stayed with me and looked at me. No, I didn't want to be shouted at again and so I ignored her. The last email was ready. I closed the notebook, leaned back and enjoyed the sun.

"Sorry for yelling right now. I was so done. The last few days have been the worst of my life." She stammered the apology and looked at me sweetly. With such a look, I could not remain dismissive. We talked and she poured her heart out to me.

Together with her boyfriend, she had saved up for the vacation and they set off together. On the way they took a hitchhiker with them. This had stretched her boyfriend out of her and would now be with her boyfriend.

Bianka, that was the name of the sweet creature sitting across from me, was simply left behind in a freeway parking lot. She had sought help without money. It was immediately grabbed by all 'friendly' helpers. Now she had been stuck here for a few days. She had found a place in the bay where she could spend the night undisturbed and today my retreat was occupied by me.

I tried to cheer Bianka up and we talked about a lot

of things. I liked the conversation and so the time passed until the sun went down. I wanted to go back to the hotel so slowly, but I was worried about Bianka. “You sleep in my hotel tonight. Tomorrow you will get a ticket from me and then you will drive home straight away. "That was a fatherly instruction, a contradiction was not possible and so Bianka followed me to the hotel in the half-light.

At the reception I put my credit card on the counter and said: "She needs a room tonight, please with breakfast." The guest book was searched by the receptionist, but she couldn't find a free room. "Then she has to go to my apartment sleep on the sofa. Please settle the cost of bed and breakfast separately. "Bianka got an access card and followed me. There was a sense of discomfort in her demeanor. The fear of being exploited again crushedher. But Bianka was so exhausted that she had given up all resistance.

The apartment had two separate rooms, bedroom and living room. So Bianka really had a room to herself. I went into the bedroom with the words that she should first take a shower and then get the bedding. I sat on the bed and turned on the television. For a long time I heard the rustling from the bathroom and then a clean, pretty, little Bianka came to get the bedding. In her cute, short nightie, she padded to the bed on her little feet, grabbed it and disappeared with a 'thank you'. I also soon lay down because I had to get up early in the morning.

The first rays of the sun woke me up. I dressed quietly and went to breakfast. When I returned to the apartment, I looked into her room and found her still in deep sleep. Too bad I couldn't say goodbye, but I still put some money in there. I wrote on a piece of paper that she should buy a ticket after breakfast and go to her parents' house.

My first meeting started soon, so I went to the company. I returned at around 7:00 p.m. As expected, the room was empty. I looked at the table, found the note and read: "Don't want the money." It said under it: "Sorry, the hunger was stronger." There was still € 95 under the slip. Bianka's backpack was packed, but it was still on the wall.

Shortly after I changed my clothes, Bianka came into the apartment. Her charming smile shone out from under the clean cap with the tied hair. She had pulled a short top over a bikini and a tight hip skirt rounded off the appearance. She came to me barefoot and gave me a kiss on the cheek.

"Nice that you're here. Are you angry that I haven't left yet? "" No, I'm hungry and so let's go eat. "

Without hesitation, she followed me to the reception and I extended her stay in the hotel. "How long should I book for the lady, a day or like her booking - until the day after tomorrow?" "Two," came from Bianka immediately shot and she looked at me innocently begging. "I'll have them put an extra bed in the room so that the lady doesn't have to lie on the uncomfortable sofa," said the woman.

So, well, word had got around from the staff that there was a young lady with me, this one but, like a daughter, slept in another bed. Well, then my reputation here in the hotel was still immaculate.

After eating in the tavern, we talked for a long time and found many things in common. It was getting very late. Back at the hotel everyone went to bed and I fell asleep immediately.

In the middle of the night I woke up and noticed how Bianka crawled under my blanket. She snuggled up to me carefully. I slipped my arm under her shoulder and pulled her lightly towards me. She immediately took the opportunity to snuggle up very closely. Her nightgown had slipped upstairs and unabashedly she pressed her shame on my leg. I clearly felt that she was not wearing anything below.

'No, I'm not a horny pervert,' I thought, trying to fall asleep. In the morning she woke up in front of me and beamed at me. Her gaze also woke me up, opened my eyes and got a kiss from her.

"You're the first one who didn't take advantage of me right away and is just kind to me." "Will you come or do you think I'm beyond good and evil?" She got the answer. "Do you seriously believe that you don't create a desire in me? As sexy as you look? As good as how can we talk? You're exactly the type of woman I want. "

She leaned on me and looked me in the eye. "Then why didn't you just do it?" "Because I'm not a horny pervert! And because I don't exploit anyone! And because I want to have mutual agreement! And because I would then no longer leave you out and then you to me forever will bind. "

I couldn't say more because she closed my mouth with a very deep kiss. I put my hands around her hips, squeezed them firmly and gently stroked her entire back.

"So, well, you either want to eat me completely or not try it at all," came from her and she disappeared into the other room to ransack the bed and get dressed.

We went to breakfast together and were observed by some work colleagues. In the company I was asked about the nice girl .. Whether it was my daughter etc. I ignored all these comments. It was the last day of the conference series and we were done around noon. So I had the whole afternoon to relax. I spent the time with Bianka in our bay.

First we lay side by side on a beach towel and talked to each other. The conversation was getting ridiculous and that day Bianka was very quick-witted. She kept provoking me until I threatened her: "I'll put you over my knee." Laughing, she jumped up and ran into the water. She called to me: "You won't get me at all." I immediately ran after her and caught her in the knee-deep water. A water battle began, in which Bianka clung to me again and again. Our bodies slid very close to each other and the wild wrangling became a tender game. Bianka nestled tightly against my body until I lifted her up and carried her to the ceiling. Here, too, she moved closer and closer to me, looking for more and more physical contact until we were closely entwined.

"I want you," Bianka whispered in my ear. "You know the consequences?" I whispered back. "They are?" "I'll take you with me tomorrow and I won't let you go." "Not a bad idea. I like it. No flirting. You want me whole, with skin and hair? "" Yes ", I couldn't say more, because my mouth was closed by a passionate kiss.

Desirably, she rubbed her abdomen against me and clearly felt my manliness. I opened her top and looked at her breasts. More than a handful, firm to touch, large atria and bean-sized hard nipples. I played around with her tongue and when I nibbled on her she moaned. She pressed her pubic firm on my bulge and suddenly it got wet between my legs. It's that fast with her, I thought, was the rubbing and the breast stimulation enough? She quickly hugged me and whispered, "Sorry, the overstimulation, it came over me like lightning." I continued to nibble on her ear and we enjoyed being close to each other.

Then I opened the ribbons of the bikini bottoms, slid my hand across the velvety pubic mound to her wet labia, and penetrated with two fingers. As if remotely controlled, she squirmed during the treatment. I led her onto the blanket to roll onto her and put my penis in front of her hole. The acorn slipped slightly between her labia, her feet immediately clasped behind my back and pulled me over. My penis slid gently into her vagina and Bianka cried out in relief. I started thrusting her and she returned every thrust so that I pushed harder and harder into her. Bianka screamed a second time, and since I didn't stop, she quickly came back to me in time. When the first shot landed in her, she gave a long cry and clawed her fingernails into my back.

"Now you are mine," I whispered and got a grumbling, "Mmm, yes".

For a long time we stayed so wrapped up and didn't care about the occasional strollers on the other end of the beach. On the way back we didn't say a word, only that Bianka was now stuck to me. Sweet togetherness does not require speech. In the hotel we changed and went to the tavern again. Today we didn't stay long and quickly returned to the hotel.

There Bianka started talking again: "You, that was wonderful. Are you always so tender or can you also access festivals? "" I can too, you will still experience it. It just has to be nice, please both and match the mood. " "I'm curious to see that there are many surprises with you and none of them made me uncomfortable." We were interrupted because her cell phone rang. With my thought, 'Why hadn't she reported to her parents in her emergency?' Bianka started the conversation.

"Hello nice that you get in touch once in a while no I couldn't, I have no credit left the ass just kicked me out at the rest area and also took the holiday allowance with us nice that he drove the car to junk probably the hitchhiker it is clear that he doesn't trust your eyes no I'm not coming home, I need too nothing I fell madly in love yes, there you can do what you want I'm three times seven he's just heavenly 40 me I can look for an apprenticeship with him, I won't find any at home anyway think about it, I'll get in touch from his phone tomorrow and if you have calmed down again we will definitely come over. Bye "Boa eye, mothers can be annoying. By the way, my ex drove into a ditch when she blew him. She's in the hospital and he's doing a gauntlet at home. "" I'm 45 and I would have to thank both of them. Without their fucking behavior I wouldn't have known you. " She hugged me and we continued talking about talking to her mother. Then she came straight to my bed and after a very long foreplay with a passionate result we fell asleep.

In the morning she first rummaged her bed, my reputation in the hotel should stay. After breakfast we packed the car and drove off. Bianka lounged in the passenger seat. She put her feet on the dashboard and her head was on my shoulder. As she continued to slide down, I said, "We only have to endure five hours or should I land in the ditch?" "I wouldn't have any problems blowing, but true, I'd rather wait five hours than land in the hospital." So she leaned against me and enjoyed it when my hand was on her thigh in between.

Suddenly she asked me: "What if I got pregnant yesterday?" "If you don't use contraception, we should get married quickly, because then I will mercilessly put a child in your stomach." The next hundred kilometers was quiet, not a word came from her. Then she said, embarrassed, "Do you like children?" "If you have as cute faces as you are, I can't get enough of them." "Thank you for the compliment. I take the pill, but at the ordeal before our meeting, I don't know if it always stayed with me. "In the further conversation, she only wanted two children, and if I was serious, then next year the bells ring. We got stuck near Osnabruck and finally, after eight hours of driving, we reached my house.

I led her through her new home and the tiredness was gone immediately. She looked enthusiastically at everything, threw herself on the bed in between, inspected the kitchen and was quickly in the garden. "You built a dream castle here." "Yes and now dragged my princess over." She jumped into my open arms and we fell together on the meadow.

While we were fooling around, my neighbor Sonja greeted us: "Well back again?" I replied to her: "Yes, but this time I brought a piece of gold with me." "But it was also time that a woman finally rules here again", and to Bianka, "If he doesn't feel, then you come over to me and after that it works." That was the nice neighbor, others probably criticized the age difference, but after a few weeks Bianka was fully accepted in the settlement.

In the evening, the first night was in the future marriage bed. We crawled under the covers and it came into my arm. Instead of falling asleep, I started to stroke and kiss her. My lips moved from her mouth, over her eyes, to her ears. I breathed in lightly and shivered Bianka ducked her head. She got goose bumps when I kissed her neck to her breasts. My lips found a new target and sucked on the nipples. I circled the firm warts with my tongue and then gently nibbled my teeth on them.

Bianka tried to dampen her vocal bursts of emotion with the pillow, but I said to her, "Scream as loud as you want. Everyone can hear you here, because everyone should know how happy we are. "From then on, she dropped without hesitation and only enjoyed her outbursts of emotion. When my tongue stuck into her belly button, she started giggling loudly, and when I was myself kissing her pubic bone, her legs flew apart like a jumping jack. In front of my eyes was the heavenly realm of pleasure. Shaved naked she felt silky and tender. Between her firm, big labia, the little ones blinked. I brushed my tongue over them big and kissed a few inches across the inside of her thighs. I hiked over the other leg again and let my tongue circle between large and small lips. Bianka screeched with delight. When I parted the small labia with my tongue and reached the clitoris, Bianka exploded and a small splash of her landed on my face.

Bianka stammered an apology, but I didn't care, and I greedily penetrated it with my tongue. My face pressed between her labia and I relished licking in her and the clitoris. Bianka was immediately in full swing again and exploded beneath me. She begged for help: "Please, please fuck me at last, push me, ram him into me, finish me off, otherwise I can't stand the request."

All good upbringing had disappeared, it was now just a bundle of nerves, a piece of meat that the lust for meat wanted to indulge in. She got what she wanted. I turned it over, started, and hit like a maniac from the start.

Squeaking with pleasure she bucked me, screamed, splashed and came back to meet the next wave. The whole thing repeated itself a few times until I discharged myself into it. Her legs buckled, she sank onto the mattress and I landed on top of her. Minutes passed, then she pushed me away so that I landed on my back next to her. She immediately began to spoil me equally.

She kissed tenderly from my mouth over my eyes to my ears. A tingling shiver ran through my entire body as she sucked on my ears. Her path continued to my neck. When her tongue roamed my nipples, I noticed that men also have sensitive nerves here. When she got to my navel, I asked her to turn around so I could touch her. Before she took care of my penis, she promptly turned so that I looked

at her buttocks and could stroke her pubes.
With relish she licked my pole, circled my acorn with her tongue and made no wrinkles. Then she lovingly took care of my sack and breathed licked over it.

I in turn had my finger in her dripping vagina, rubbed her clit and kept pushing the mucus to her anus. When I started massaging the hole with my thumb, Bianka's tongue moved to my hole. After initially gently licking, she pressed her tongue firmly against it. So my cock got rock hard again and I also pressed my thumbs in her butt. Bianka immediately jerked back and made a cat hump. But she came back quickly and pressed her butt against me, so that the thumb slid into the hole. I gently massaged her sphincter while Bianka put her head on my stomach and gently sucked on my penis. The massage twitched the sphincter rhythmically, but the pressure quickly became weaker. The hole slowly widened and could pick up two fingers.
Bianka pressed my butt towards me, but otherwise remained stiff and waited for the things to come. When she got used to two fingers, she let my stiff out of her mouth and said: "If you want to deflower me there, please be careful."

I sat up, knelt behind her and she made a hollow

back. I first pushed my penis into her slippery vagina to lubricate it and then switched to her butt. I slowly pressed against the sphincter and Bianka lightly pressed against it. A squeak came from her and the acorn had passed. I stayed in the position. I felt a pulsating pressure on my limb, but the pressure decreased and Bianka pushed towards me. That was also the command for me to push further into it and so penetrate as far as it would go. The slight pressure had now turned into a counterpressure and Bianka enjoyed the filling. Slowly I pulled back to get back to the stop and with every push Bianka sucked in the air. She slowly got used to the feeling and supported me with the movement, so I increased the pace until my testicle clapped against her pussy with every push. Because of the tightness and the incredible feeling it came to me. I injected deep into her gut and fell wearily on Bianka. She tipped aside with me.

So we stayed, my cock was held by the sphincter and Bianka nestled her butt against me. When I got enough air again, she moved her butt again and enjoyed the feeling of anal filling. The sphincter had squeezed the blood into my penis so that it didn't go limp and was still rock-hard filling her gut.

"That was good. What else do you do with me? "" Everything you allow, but only that. " "Ok try everything you want. Now I want to be taken from the beginning again. "

I pulled him out, lay down on Bianka, and pushed forward. Her legs were immediately on my shoulder and I pounded on her. Now my testicle slapped against the battered butt and Bianka screamed with delight. She reared up several times in an orgasm frenzy, but I did not slow down when she was already limp below me, grinning my eyes and stepping away. When it came to me, she still felt my injection. With the last of her strength she hugged me and pulled me down to her. I also hugged Bianka in my arms and we fell asleep together.

We had often done it together this weekend, so Bianka literally walked around with wide legs. The neighbors had also heard a lot, because envious looks came over to us. The following week I had to work again and Bianka quickly became the perfect housewife. She did everything fairly quickly and could even lie in the sun all afternoon in the garden. Every evening I noticed that she grew more beautiful every day. Did that work at all? She was pretty at the beginning. I was definitely in love with her.

The following year we got married and Bianka got pregnant. I hoped it would be a girl and I got my wish fulfilled.

The End.

STORY 8

I was a software engineer for a medium-sized German company that had recently moved its development department to other European countries.

Fortunately, for me, not to Southeast Europe but to Ireland. The other colleagues would rather have ended up in Italy, Greece or Hungary. There, they said, the weather would be better. I personally found Ireland better. The weather was entertaining, varied and never boring. The people were nice, the beer (ok, I didn't like Guinness) good, the whiskey if you didn't overdo it, too.

I have rarely visited Germany since I moved to Ireland. Somehow I only phoned my mother. After my father ran away with another, my mother lived alone in my old hometown, but did not want to leave because of the friends.

One day I had to go to Germany for a week on business trip to the company headquarters. Since I haven't had a girlfriend in Ireland for half a year, the old one wanted to marry, which was not my cup of tea, so I thought that I would treat myself to something.

I didn't know much about the city I was in, but what

were taxi drivers and hotel porters for?

I got a list of different shops with rentable and usable women from both sides, checked the Internet again for what was known about these shops, and then took a taxi to a shop, which both interviewed and the Internet said that it would not be very cheap, but the ladies were solid.

I was warmly received there and asked if I had a preference, they currently had an 18 year old that they could offer me in school uniform, or, as an upper limit, a 44 year old who would act as a teacher. I could also have both, together.

They would also have a very special offer, if I liked one of the ladies, I could have them for me for a whole week.

I say that I would like to have an overview of the currently available possibilities, whether that would be possible, which of course was done. The ladies were shown to me, and one of them caught my eye because that was my mother. When she saw me, she wanted to hide behind the others, but I said to the "lady of the house" that I wanted exactly this woman, my mother.

So my mother, who was wearing very sharp

clothing, had to come to my table. A corset that left the breasts completely free, on the corset, which also served as a garter belt, two sharp stockings, high-heeled shoes on the feet, no panties. It was just awesome, my mother's face said that if I even made a sound, she would kill me.

I looked at the lady of the house, she gave me a room number, and both of us, my mother and I, went into this room.

As soon as the door was closed, she wanted me to disappear immediately, whereupon I said, "And what will your boss say if the customer leaves immediately? Or should I tell her that you are my mother?" What she didn't want again, I showed on the bed, she lay down, I sat next to it and took a closer look at my mother. Beautiful, non-sagging breasts with nipples that were nice and thick, a shaved pussy with labia that were thick and full, a clit that could be seen that you were enjoying yourself.

Suddenly she said "Don't look at me like this, I'm your mother", my answer was "At the moment you are the hooker I chose", which she acknowledged with a red head.

Then she wondered how she would get into this

profession and why she would live here now, and no longer in my hometown. Then she said that after my father left, she no longer had a husband, but over time she got hornier. So she went to different swinger clubs. And it was always more fun to fuck with the different men. Then when the money became a little bit scarce, my father did not always or even regularly pay child support, and without a job my mother had no other income, she had thought that a job as a hooker, in a good puff, would best suit her current needs would do justice.

She'd been doing this job for three months now, and would never have come across surprising (looking at me) and uncomfortable customers.

I started undressing and she asked what that was about. I said I paid, so I want something for my money.

Then she said, "OK, only with a condom, no blowing, no ass fuck", I asked "Riding? Nipple-sucking? Kissing?", The answer was "Yes, no, no". Onmy last question "with or without orgasm?" she said "just try it".

So I started, first the good old missionary position where I could look her in the eye. They became a little more restless, then I turned around so that she rode on me and I twirled her nipples. Here her breathing became a little faster. Shortly before I came I turned her back on and started again. Her breath became more restless, her eyes more unfocused and stiff, and when I splashed into the lump bag, it came to her too. Quite violent.

Then I lay down next to her. She lay there, I washed and went downstairs. There I told the puff mother that I wanted to have this woman all week, I would take her with me straight away. As long as my mother wasn't downstairs, I called the hotel and changed my room to a double room. With a single room bill and a second one for the surcharge. This seems to be more common with this hotel, there were no problems.

My mother came down, looked at me, why I was still there, I hung up and the puff mother said to my mother, "The gentleman takes you a whole week, get dressed." My mother stared at me, started to open her mouth, turned and disappeared.

After 10 minutes she stood in front of me dressed normally, I took her hand and we went.

Outside, she broke free and asked what this nonsense was about, and I replied that she had just bought herself for a whole week. It would belong the entire 7 days, 24 hours. Just me, you completely. She stared at me, I took her hand and we drove to the hotel.

When we were in my room she took off her coat and stood in front of me in her puff clothes. Then I said, that's not how it works. I couldn't take her to where I wanted to take her in these clothes, so I told her to put her on and took her out again.

I called a taxi outside and let us drive to her apartment. There I told her to pack normal clothes for a week, which she did. I said to the bedding "It doesn't need it, we sleep naked", which brought me a bad look again.

When she stood in front of me in normal clothes she looked like a very smart 44 year old. With that you could be seen everywhere. Even in the company.

So we drove back to the hotel, put the suitcase down and went to a fine restaurant for dinner.

I did small talk, asked her what music she liked to listen to, which films she would like to see, whether, in her job, she only blushed slightly, because a private evening was possible at all (which she denied), what literature she did would read and all that stuff, with which one passes the time and wants to convince the woman that one would not like to sit naked in front of her.

We went back to the hotel, when I went to bed I asked her which side she preferred, she looked weird, I said "right or left, not up or down", which made her laugh. The answer to the right was so we went to the bathroom one by one and lay down in our half of the bed. I turned her briefly to her, gave her a kiss on the mouth, said good night, and soon fell asleep.

The next morning I woke up to see my mother looking at me. I looked back, she pulled back her covers, I could see her whole, bare body, and she asked "how do I like you?". My answer was "spicy, if you were not my mother I would never give you away", then I flipped back my blanket and started to crawl over it and then, without a bag, put my cock in her pussy and she to fuck. I kissed her. She got two orgasms before I had mine going into her.

We lay next to each other for a while, then I got up and said, "I have to go to the company and be back at 4:30 pm, stay decent mom".

In the company I had to think about her again and again when I arrived at the hotel, she just came back, probably from shopping, because she had some expensive looking bags with her.

We spent the whole week together, slept with each other, fucked each other, fucked each other. Once we were in the opera, she in a sharp dress, without bra and panties, when we came out of the opera, she said that she absolutely had to be fucked, she was too horny, which I of course liked to do immediately. Then we went, she with full pussy, in a fine restaurant. First she grabbed the cloth napkin and put it in her crotch so that "the sauce" shouldn't run out and leave marks in the dress.

When we left she put the soaked napkin on the table. The week was nice.
On the last day, just before my "rental period" ended, I asked her if she would come to Ireland with me. Since she would have adopted her maiden name, nobody would know that we would be mother and son if we lived together in my apartment.

Then she looked surprised, said that she had to think about it, and disappeared from my life again.

When I was at work on Monday, the phone rang, it was the reception below. There would be a woman there who absolutely had to speak to me.

I went downstairs and there she was, my mother, my beloved mother. With a car in front of the door and all your luggage. She just packed everything up on Friday and would have left (driving left is not that easy with a continental car, she told me with a laugh).

I gave her my apartment keys and called the tenant downstairs to receive "my friend".

I've been living in Ireland with my lover for five years, we don't want to leave. The neighbors always ask when we would finally get married, and she always replies, "If I get my son's permission. He's against having a stepfather who is as old as he is," and everyone has to laugh .

Somehow that's right, I just can't imagine being my own stepfather. The End.

STORY 10

Oh god I love these breasts. Bhiankha is the name of my personal porn crush. For weeks, I've only been bringing one down to her. Bhiankha is a Colombian sex cam model with the hottest breasts I've ever seen. Her 80G bust was the highlight of my fantasies. Of course, they were a little big, but that didn't make them less attractive. The coolest thing about her breasts was her enormously long nipples, which were thick and long like fingertips from her nipples.

Bhiankha didn't actually do much when she did her shows, but she captivated me. As a rule, she appeared in lingerie in which you could see her breasts. She masturbated with her hand or a vibrator or massaged her huge breasts from which she squirted breast milk.

I watched Bhiankha milk the milk from her nipple and groan. I had my cock unpacked and was jerking myself off wildly when Bhiankha thanked her fans who complimented her. I imagined myself sucking on her big nipple and drinking her milk. I fantasized so much about her that I didn't even notice how the door to my room opened.

"Oh dear God. Luke!" shouted my mother, who

burst into my room.

I immediately threw my cell phone to the side, on which the film with Bhiankha was running, and covered my cock with a blanket. My mother looked at my phone, which was still showing Bhiankha's milk spurting boobs.

"What did I tell you about masturbation?" she dived angrily and went to the bed to take my cell phone in hand and turn it off. I know exactly what she said about masturbation. My mother has been highly religious since my father died and masturbation was a sin for her.

"I told you not to do that. It's forbidden! The male semen belongs in a woman's lap!"

"I know," I said, rolling my eyes.

"You don't take this seriously! It is the third time that I have caught you. You will go to hell for that!"

"I know mom," I repeated.

"Why are you doing this? Can't you keep control until you get married? Then you can do all of this with a real woman!"

"Mom, it's 2017. It's not like you introduce me to a woman within a week and then we get married."

"God's commandments still apply in another thousand years! These are all excuses. I just want that we are all later united in heaven," said she and sat down on the bed. It was a really uncomfortable situation to be touched by her while my erection did not swell under the covers.

"Mom, I can't help it. It just has to ... get out." She looked at me sympathetically.
"I know it's hard for you, but do it for me. For mom" Somehow strange to have to promise not to masturbate for her.
"I can promise you so many times, mom, but I will always have to disappoint you."

She thought for a moment. "Can I help you?" she asked. "How are you going to help me?" I asked unsuspectingly.
"Masturbation is murder. Murder is a mortal sin and I can't let you do it." "And what do you suggest?"
"You could help with a smaller, less bad sin?"

"Which would be?" I asked skeptically.

"Sex before marriage," she said, looking down at herself. "Great. And with whom?" I asked unsuspectingly.
"With me"

"But that would be incest! Isn't it worse?"

"Better than murder, right? If you absolutely need it, I could help you. Sex before marriage is a sin, but it doesn't harm me. God will know that it is the best solution."

"Mom, I don't think we should do that."

"You have a choice: either you promise to stop it or you will do it with me in the future."

"And you wouldn't have a problem doing it with your own son?" I asked.

"Not if I can help you," she said, running her finger over her cleavage. "Besides, I've been pretty lonely since your father passed away ..."
My mother really offered me to do it with me? Or was it just a weird test? "So? What do you say? Do you want to sin with your mother?"

I don't know what had ridden me. Maybe I was just so horny and thought too much about Bhiankha's hot nipples, but I nodded to my mother. She got up and left my room without a word. I was still sitting excited and thinking about what had happened. Was my reaction wrong? Should I have refused? It was clear to me that sex with my own mother was not a much better alternative than masturbation. At least morally. Or well, was it much worse? Would we harm anyone with it? I was really confused. I had never thought about incest in my life and now I didn't know what to make of it. At least until the moment my mother came through the door again.

My mother stood in the door in sexy underwear: black lace bra, suspenders and suspenders with black lace stockings. I was surprised at how sexy my mother was. I immediately got a hard erection again. I was particularly taken with her bulging bra and her missing panties and thus a look at her bare pussy.

"I hope you like it. I haven't worn it in ages."

"Mom, you look wonderful," I said, hoping not to drool. "So?" she asked. "Are you ready for sin?" "Yes, mother," I said, watching her walk up to me and climb onto my bed. She pulled the blanket from my legs and immediately reached for my hard cock. She slowly pushed my foreskin back and forth and watched my cock closely. She even started to breathe deeper. She slid closer to me and put her lips over my glans.

"Oh god" I shrugged and enjoyed her tongue on my cock.

She sucked him passionately and I had to hold back from coming. I was a virgin and it was a completely new feeling for me.

Then she sat up and sat on my legs. I felt her warm pussy on my testicles, but she didn't sit on my cock yet.

"Are you ready?"

"Yes, mom," I groaned. Then she led my acorn to her labia and lowered her hips. Bit by bit my cock penetrated my mother. I clutched my bed sheet and tried to endure it. It felt insane.

My mother went up and down with her hip and started riding me. Suddenly she groaned loudly: "Our Father in heaven, ..."

She went up with her hips until I was barely in her. Only my acorn was stuck between her labia and threatened to slip out. "...Blessed be your name."

Then she slid down my bar until she literally sat like the hen on my eggs. I was as deep as possible in my mother, who groaned more and more heavily: "... your kingdom COME"

She emphasized the word "coming" as an allusion and I had to pull myself together in order not to do that. "... your will be done"

My will happened because I wanted nothing more than to be in my mother, who leaned forward slightly and offered me an even better look at her breasts.

"... like in heaven, so on earth" she moaned louder and faster and increased the speed at which she rode me. I was in heaven on earth, I thought to myself.

"... give us our daily bread today ..." she moaned and I was focused on her breasts, which looked great in her bra, but I wished I could see them all. Bhiankha's tits were still in the back of my head and I wondered if my mother's breasts could keep up.

"...

Fuck it all. Forgive me my guilt, mom, I thought, and grabbed her bra to pull it down a bit. Under it, my mother hid a pair of beautiful breasts with hard nipples that longed to be sucked again. They weren't Oschis like Bhiankha's, but big enough that I had to squeeze my face into my mother's bosom to suck on her nipples.

"... how we forgive our guilty parties," she moaned

and leaned forward. She pressed my breasts into my face and moaned even louder when I started sucking on them like a little baby.

"And don't lead us ... Aaaah ..."

Her moans grew stronger and she had to start over again. "And lead us not into temptation..."

Too late, I thought. I was tempted. From my own mother. I sucked her breast very hard and truly prayed to God that milk would flow out of him like Bhiankha's tits. How perverse would it be to let my mother breastfeed while she fucks me?

"... but deliver and from evil," she groaned and straightened up again. I immediately grabbed her hot tits that jiggled while riding and massaged them tightly.

"... Because yours is the kingdom and the strength and the glory forever" I heard her almost finish the Lord's Prayer when she rode me wilder. "Now come to mom's chest," she groaned.

I immediately straightened up and sucked on her nipple. "Give me your seed, my boy.
She clutched me tightly and pressed my face very close to her chest so that I could hardly breathe. She stroked my hair and groaned in my ear.

"Mom, mom, I'm coming!" I groaned this time. "Come on, my son. Spray me full"
And so it happened. I sprayed a full jug and could have come a second time thinking that I was jerking off the pussy that gave birth to me. It was the ultimate taboo. "Amen" groaned my mother.

"Amen," I replied from my breath.

My mother stood by me and let me fall back into my bed. "God will forgive us," said she. "I never want to see you masturbate again. Just come to mom, okay?"

"OK" I groaned exhausted and grinned. My mother was an angel!

The End.

CPSIA information can be obtained
at www.ICGtesting.com
Printed in the USA
BVHW090438190521
607644BV00014B/1766

9 781801 872751